minedition

English edition published 2018 by Michael Neugebauer Publishing Ltd., Hong Kong

Text copyright © 2018 by Patricia de Arias
Illustration copyright © 2018 by Laura Borràs
Original title: EI Camino de Marwan
Copyright © Amanuta, Chile 2016
Coproduction with Michael Neugebauer Publishing Ltd., Hong Kong.
This English edition is published by arrangement with Amanuta
through The ChoiceMaker Korea Co.
Michael Neugebauer Publishing Ltd.,
Unit 28, 5/F, Metro Centre, Phase 2,No.21 Lam Hing Street, Kowloon Bay, Kowloon, Hong Kong.
Phone +852 2807 1711, e-mail: info@minedition.com
This edition was printed in July 2017 at L.Rex Printing Co Ltd.
3/F., Blue Box Factory Building, 25 Hing Wo Street, Tin Wan, Aberdeen, Hong Kong, China
Typesetting in Iowa Old Style Roman
Library of Congress Cataloging-in-Publication Data available upon request.

ISBN 978-988-8341-55-9
10 9 8 7 6 5 4 3 2 1
First Impression

For more information please visit our website: www.minedition.com

MARWAN'S JOURNEY

Patricia de Arias
Illustrated by Laura Borràs

minedition

I take giant steps
even though I am small.

One,
two,
three...
crossing
the desert.

I walk, and my footsteps leave a trace of ancient stories, the songs of my homeland, and the smell of tea and bread, jasmine and earth.

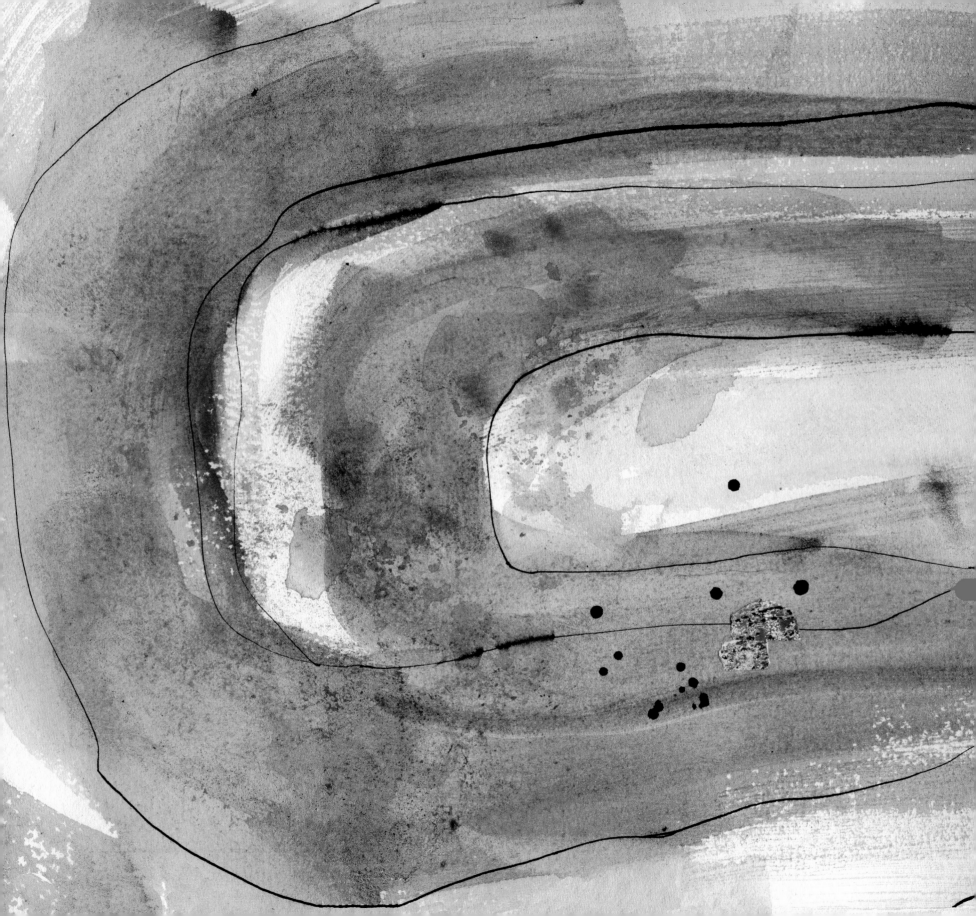

I walk...
and I don't know
when I will get there,
or where I am going.
I carry a heavy bag.

My mended clothing, a prayer book,
a notebook, a pencil, a photograph of my mommy.

Sometimes, in the cold night, I cry out to her in my dreams.
She comes with her black hair streaming, and tucks me in
with her flour-soft hands.

She says:

Marwan, keep going, walk, and walk, and walk.

And I keep walking.

I remember a house. Mommy lit the fire when night fell, and Daddy told stories of our homeland. There was a garden, a cat and a ray of sunlight that shone every morning on my pillow.

One night they came...
The darkness grew colder, deeper, darker,
and swallowed up everything:
my house, my garden, my homeland.

After that we walked
for one day,
two,
three...

Hundreds of people, thousands of feet, one in front of the other.

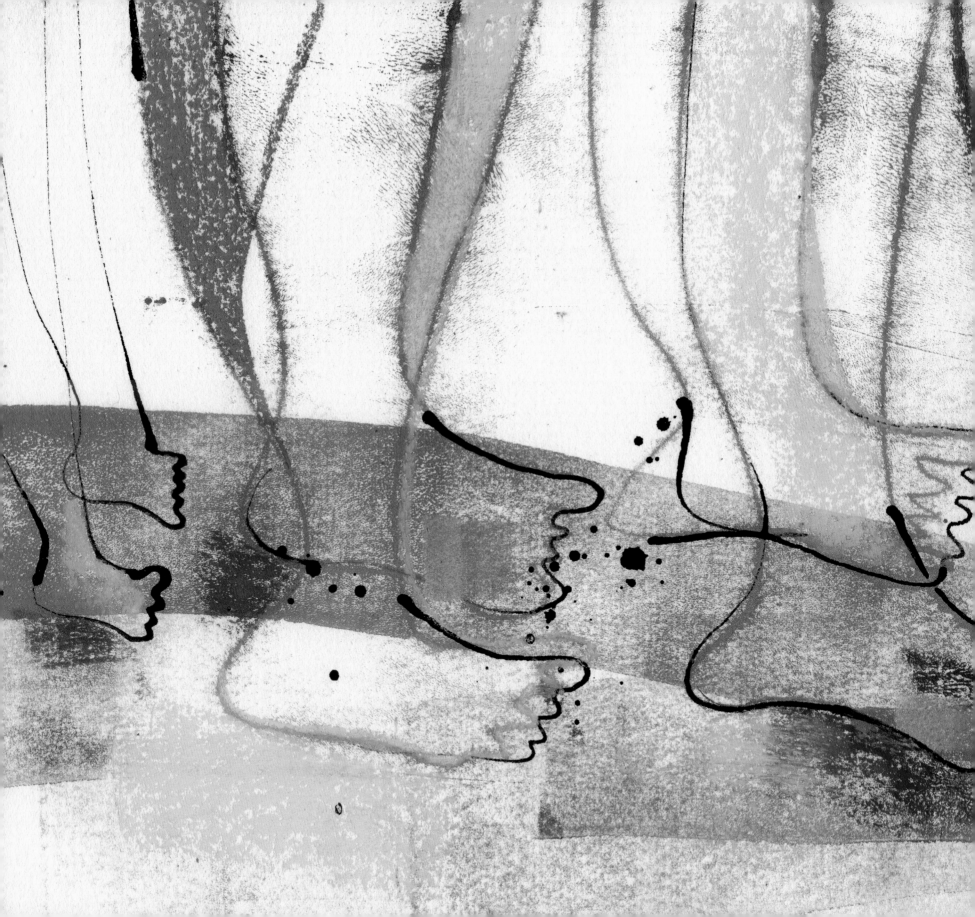

One...
two...
three...

A line of humans like ants
crossing the desert.
Marwan, keep walking,
don't look back...

And I don't look back.

Ahead lies
the border.
They say that it is
an infinite line
that separates the
desert from the sea.

Another country, another house,
another language.

Stories of other homelands.

One day, I will return.
I will not hesitate.

I will plant a garden with my hands,
full of flowers and hope.

I will build my house with the cement of my sure steps.

I will let in the rays of sunlight that come
through the windows and paint the walls
with happiness.

Every night I will pray that the night never, never, never goes so dark again.